The *Princess* AND THE GOD

A RICHARD JACKSON BOOK

The Princess AND THE GOD

by Doris Orgel

ORCHARD BOOKS   NEW YORK

Orchard Books
95 Madison Avenue
New York, NY 10016

Manufactured in the United States of America
Book design by Jean Krulis
The text of this book is set in 13 point Bembo.

10 9 8 7 6 5 4 3 2 1

Library of Congress Cataloging-in-Publication Data
Orgel, Doris.
   The princess and the god / by Doris Orgel.
     p. cm.
   "A Richard Jackson book"—Half t.p.
   Summary: Princess Psyche's beauty incurs the wrath of the goddess Venus
who sends her son Cupid to seek revenge.
   ISBN 0-531-09516-9.—ISBN 0-531-08866-9 (lib. bdg.)
   1. Psyche (Greek deity)—Juvenile fiction. 2. Cupid (Roman deity)—
Juvenile fiction. 3. Venus (Roman deity)—Juvenile fiction. [1. Psyche (Greek
deity)—Fiction. 2. Cupid (Roman deity)—Fiction. 3. Venus (Roman
deity)—Fiction. 4. Mythology, Classical—Fiction.] I. Title.
PZ7.0632Pr 1996   [Fic]—dc20   95-33527

For Shelley

The
Princess
AND THE
GOD

I ⚜

The others in the procession turned back when the footpath ended. Only my father and I climbed on. We reached the height where no trees grew. We clambered up the steepening slope all the way to the barren summit.

A north wind howled around us. The sharp, thin air made breathing painful. My father took my face in his hands and said, "If only I had not gone to Miletus . . ."

I'd never seen him weep before. I touched my finger to his cheek, caught a tear rolling down, put it to my lips. I said, "Father, it is not your

fault. My fate would have found me all the same."
I sounded braver than I felt. I clasped my arms
around him, clutched him tight.

My father prayed to Venus: "Goddess born
of the foam, relent toward my child." He waved
the words seaward. He kissed me for the last time.
I loosened my arms from around him. Hunching
up his shoulders like a lonely old, grief-stricken
man, he began the long way down.

Soon I could not see him anymore.

Heavy storm clouds rolled above me, darken-
ing the sky. The biting wind blew through my
wedding veil, made billows of my gown. I shivered from the cold, and from my fear. What mortal would not have been afraid?

But I would not cower. The fate I was about
to face, however terrifying, was mine alone.
Therefore I resolved to embrace it. When the
dragon bridegroom came, he would find me
ready.

Once, years ago, we were three little princesses
in my father's kingdom. My two sisters, Procne
and Petra, were pretty, as princesses are meant to

be. Of me, the youngest, people said, "Psyche is beautiful beyond compare."

Was it true?

I asked my old nurse. She had cared for me since my mother died, when I was small.

"Look in the mirror," she answered.

The mirror showed me deep green eyes, a high, smooth forehead, a mass of curly red-brown hair with glints of gold.

My nurse said, "Thank the gods for what you see."

But my sisters whispered secrets behind my back and would not let me play with them.

My nurse said, "They are envious of your beauty."

I was ten, still a child. I prayed to the gods, "Please make me plain."

One time I put splotches of mud on my face and stuck burrs in my hair to make myself look ugly. I ran to my sisters and asked, "Now will you let me play with you?"

But they still would not, and only laughed at me.

My nurse tugged the burrs loose, scrubbed my face till it stung, and scolded, "Don't you know that when you scorn the gods' gifts, they will take revenge?"

One day while I was gathering walnuts in the palace garden, I sensed that I was being watched. When I stood up, I saw a group of townspeople outside the fence. They pressed their faces between the bars and gaped at me. I hid behind the thickest tree and would not come out till the last of them was gone.

But the next day more people came, and more every day, waiting for glimpses of me.

I tried to stay in groves and thickets hidden from view. But sometimes my ball or my hoop would roll away. Or else, forgetting for a moment, I'd run or skip out into the open. And there they would be, behind the fence, shouting, "Princess beyond compare, show us your beautiful face!" Then I'd run and hide as fast as I could, wishing they'd let me be.

One time a man shouted, "No mortal can be so beautiful!"

My nurse, never far from my side, clapped her hands over my ears to shield me from blasphemy, but I heard it all the same: "That is not our princess; that is Venus herself! Beautiful goddess, be gracious to us!"

4

"No," protested an older, white-bearded man, "that *is* our princess Psyche, but she is more beautiful than even the goddess Venus. Therefore let us worship her." The whole crowd fell to their knees.

"Go! Leave us in peace!" called my nurse in her quivery old voice. They took no notice.

Our palace guards shooed them away, but only for a while.

My father ordered more guards around the palace. He sent officials to reason with the crowds. He went out among them himself and pleaded, "Good people, you deceive yourselves. Princess Psyche is human, the same as you and I. If you do her too great honor, you will anger the gods. It is they you must worship, not my beloved youngest child."

Priests and priestesses added their warnings. But ever greater crowds came, bringing flower garlands, loaves and cakes baked of the season's first grains—gifts they should have offered to Venus. Her altars fell into neglect.

My sisters called me "little goddess" and pretended to be amused by it all. But my nurse said, "Secretly they would give anything if crowds would come and worship *them* instead."

Procne was the eldest. Soon she would turn fifteen, the age when maidens in our kingdom could be wooed. Weeks before her birthday feast, she and Petra started to scan the horizon for ships that might bring suitors.

When the first such ship docked in our harbor, Procne tried on all her elegant gowns and jewelry. Petra helped her to decide which to wear. Then they noticed me watching and clucked their tongues. "Poor little Venus," they said. "When it's your turn, no suitors will come."

"Why not?" I asked.

"Because mortals would not dare to ask for the hand of a 'goddess' in marriage," they answered gleefully.

Procne's suitors were kings and princes from near and far. They ranged in appearance from handsome to ill formed, and in years from younger than she to older than our father. Most came from kingdoms comparable to our father's in size and wealth.

Procne and Petra discussed them all in great detail. My bedroom was next to theirs. I heard them talking till late in the night, comparing the suitors' every feature and making guesses about what each one's palace and possessions were worth.

Procne sighed and said, "Oh, why cannot the handsomest also be the richest?"

And Petra said, in a little-girl voice, "But Sister, aren't there certain secret ways to foretell which will make the best, most *pleasing* husband?" Then they tittered knowingly and lowered their voices to whispers.

Finally Procne decided on the suitor from the richest realm. He was three times her age, bald as an egg, and seldom smiled. I thought perhaps she had some special fondness for him.

"I do, I do," she said. "Don't try to understand it. You're still a child. You can't know about such things." She sounded in earnest. But then she glanced at Petra, and they broke into laughter.

The day after the wedding, she sailed off with her new husband to be queen over his important, wealthy land.

The following year it was Petra's turn to choose among her suitors. Having no one else to talk with, she boasted to me how handsome, rich, and attentive they were.

I could see that she did not care for any of them.

She chose a king from a realm not far from Procne's. He flattered her most charmingly. But he was fat as an ox.

Watching her sail away to her new life, I promised myself that I would choose differently, should suitors come for me.

As the only princess left, I missed my sisters' nearness, their chattering and laughter. But most of all I missed the hope to which I'd clung while we three were still under the same roof: that they would soften toward me, include me in their affections.

Meantime the crowds of gapers kept growing. Throughout the kingdom people had come to believe I was a goddess. Even servants in our palace who'd known me all my life and saw me every day believed it. Those my own age, even former playmates, kept a worshipful distance. Soon I had no one I could talk to except my old nurse, who was gloomy and filled with foreboding, and my father, whom I did not wish to burden with my loneliness lest it deepen his own.

My fifteenth birthday approached.

From the parapet of our palace roof, you could

see the harbor. I often went up there. I'd stand leaning over and scan the horizon. When a sail came into view, I imagined a stately ship and on it a suitor pacing to and fro, impatient to ask for my hand in marriage. I told myself that my sisters' prediction could well have been mistaken, and dreamed up many suitors to my liking.

None came.

One time my nurse, after searching all over, ran huffing and puffing up the stairs and cried, "No, Psyche, don't! The gods give us little enough time on earth!" She pulled me away from the parapet, thinking I'd meant to throw myself over. She cradled me in her arms, smoothed my hair, wept, and sighed, "Ah, the pity, to be wrongly worshiped, who rightfully should be wooed."

More and more, I gave myself to daydreams. I pieced together in my mind hints from paintings on our palace walls, from certain books in my father's library, and, not least, from signs my body sent me. In this way I tried to imagine how it might be to love a husband who in turn loved me. But the more vividly I envisioned it, the sadder I grew, for the clearer it seemed that such happiness was not to be.

My father was troubled and perplexed. How could he set things right? A philosopher who'd been his tutor when he was young had taught him that beauty was an outward sign of inner truth and that the gods rewarded it. My father placed much trust in the gods, particularly in Apollo. He thought he could find the answer by sailing to Miletus and consulting Apollo's oracle there.

"No! Not that!" my nurse cried when she heard about it. She feared and mistrusted the gods. No god, nor goddess either, had intervened when warriors had carried her off and sold her into slavery as a small child. Ever since then, she'd had visions and dreams about the pain and suffering that the gods inflicted on humans, simply to amuse themselves.

She knelt before my father. She hugged his knees. "Don't go, my lord," she begged, shaking and trembling, but she could not change his mind. He sailed for Miletus.

I waited anxiously for his return. When finally I spied his ship on the horizon, I ran to the harbor to greet him.

He embraced me, but in silence. He would

not tell me what the Pythoness, priestess of the oracle, had said.

Not till we entered the palace did my father speak. And then it was not his own voice, but the Pythoness's ancient, impassive croaking that came from his lips: "When Psyche's sixteenth birthday dawns, let her put on wedding clothes. Bring her to your kingdom's highest mountain peak. There a dragon bridegroom, feared even by the gods, will claim her for his own."

Hearing those words, my old nurse fell to the floor in a faint. We carried her to her bed. I kept watch as she lay unconscious. Her face twitched. She moaned. I thought perhaps some god or goddess was sending her a vision of my fate.

II ⁓❦⁓

Many thousands of years before Psyche was born, when the world was still new, gods and goddesses moved freely among humans. In that time, a brave young man named Peleus won the love of the sea goddess Thetis, and they married. Countless deities came to the wonderful wedding feast: the mighty ones from Mount Olympus and the lesser ones of forests, fields, and water. The only one not wanted was Eris, twin sister of the war god, Mars, for wherever she set foot, quarrels followed.

Eris was bitterly offended. She swore she would take revenge.

She came to the feast uninvited, bringing a won-

drous golden apple with these words emblazoned on it: "For the fairest."

She rolled it to the feet of three goddesses standing close together: Juno, queen of Olympus; wise Minerva, skilled in battle; and Venus, who ruled over passionate desire.

Each goddess thought the apple was meant for her.

All three bent down to claim it. But Peleus feared their quarreling would spoil the wedding feast. So he snatched it away and gave it to Jupiter, king of the gods, for safekeeping.

To whom did it rightly belong?

Jupiter was husband to Juno. Therefore he could not be impartial and put off making a decision.

Long after the wedding feast, the apple was still in his keeping. Finally he gave it to a human he favored, a prince of Troy named Paris. He appointed Paris to judge who most deserved it and then called Juno, Minerva, and Venus to appear before him.

No sooner did they arrive than they whispered promises into young Paris's ear:

"If you judge me the fairest, I will make you the mightiest ruler on earth," promised Juno.

"If you judge me the fairest, I will fight by your side and bring you victory in every battle," promised Minerva.

And Venus whispered, "You know very well who the fairest is. Give me the prize, and the most beautiful woman on earth shall be yours."

Paris gazed at them a long while. He admired Juno's milk-white arms and Minerva's flashing eyes, her high, smooth brow. But Venus's luminous perfection left him breathless, and he placed the apple in her hands.

Soon afterward, just as Venus had promised, Paris won the most beautiful woman on earth. She was Helen, queen of Sparta. He stole her away from her husband, King Menelaus, thereby starting a famous and bloody war, the one at Troy.

Venus brought the golden apple to her favorite earthly dwelling. She gave it a place of honor atop a marble pedestal, and there it stayed.

One day, many thousands of years later, the goddess took it down. She inspected it closely but found not a scratch or blemish. The apple shone. "For the fairest" blazed forth as brightly as when she had first cast eyes on it.

But Venus had heard tell of a mortal, a mere girl, stealing away her worshipers. And she wondered, Am I still the fairest?"

She sent a servant to bring a mirror. She examined

her reflection minutely. I seem as I always was, she thought, unless the mirror is clouded. Or is it that my eyes no longer see quite clearly?

She called her son Cupid to come to her.

He was then a boyish, prankish god whose chief pleasure was shooting arrows at fellow gods and humans, whomever his mother or he himself decreed.

An obedient son, he came quickly to his mother's side.

"Is Olympus in upheaval?" Venus asked. "Has Jupiter fallen to a superior might, and are we goddesses and gods now subject to change and decay?"

"Of course not, Mother. Why would you think such a thing?"

"Look at me. Am I the same?"

Cupid laid his head on Venus's bosom, smiled up at her, and answered, "Yes. You are as fair today as you were on the day you arose from the sea, the fairest goddess that ever graced the world."

"Then how is it that my temples and shrines are neglected, abandoned, and my former worshipers now pray to a girl, a mere mortal?"

"What mortal, Mother?"

"Come, take my hand. I'll show you."

They made themselves invisible and flew to Psyche's garden.

They hovered over a stone bench on which she sat. She was plucking petals from a daisy and throwing them away like so many abandoned hopes of ever finding love.

Cupid drew in his breath and murmured, "She is lovely!"

Crowds stood outside the fence and shouted, "Most beautiful princess, our new Venus, show yourself!"

"Did you hear that?" The true Venus shook her fists. "Cupid, avenge your mother. Put a stop to this!"

"Yes, yes," he muttered, feasting his eyes on Psyche.

Venus pulled an arrow from his quiver, placed it in his hand. "Hurry! Take aim! Inflame her with a passion for the crudest, meanest fool in this whole kingdom."

The crowd went on shouting praises to Psyche.

"Do not fail me," Venus said. "I can bear it no longer. Farewell."

She hoped to find comfort in the sea that had given her birth, and she willed herself to a shore nearby.

She dipped her toes in the lacelike foam the shallow ripples left on the sand. She strode out to where the waves rolled wildly. They grew tame beneath her, allowing her to tread on them, leap from one to the other, for as long and as far as she pleased. Finally,

16

when the shore was no longer in sight, she plunged down into the depths.

Nereids, shimmering mermaid-goddesses, and their Triton brothers swam to her and greeted her with songs and conch-shell blasts.

Azure-bearded Neptune, his queen, Amphitrite, and their small son, Palaemon, came forth from their palace, which stood on the dry ground of the sea, and invited her to ride in their chariot with them.

Six strong Tritons yoked together lifted the chariot from below and carried it to the surface. There it glided smoothly. Playful dolphins swam along, now diving down, now leaping up companionably.

Venus petted their glistening faces. She took deep, soothing breaths of the fragrant salt air. She trailed her hand through the crystal-clear water. Enjoying all these pleasures, she regained her composure and put her anger aside—but not for long.

III ⁓

All was quiet around me. The north wind had died down. The only sounds I heard were the beats of my heart. Suddenly another wind whirled toward me from the west. It swept me up with mighty gusts and carried me aloft.

Was it my bridegroom's messenger, come to deliver me into his clutches? Or was it he, himself? Would he now reveal his dragon form, devour me in midflight? Or would he bring me to his lair and only then sink his claws and teeth into my flesh?

Whatever power had me in its grasp drove the

clouds racing across the sky. It carried me higher and higher. How strange to leave the earth so far behind and yet be still alive.

The mountain peak was shrouded in mist, as though it had put on a mourning veil in sorrow over me. Mountain peak, last place on earth where my feet stood, good-bye. Clouds, and sky, and air I breathed, good-bye. Good-bye, my childhood, my girlhood, my womanhood unattained. Good-bye to the loving I'd dreamed of and would never know.

I drew deep breaths, prepared to breathe my last. Yet, strangely, I did not weep and was not sad. A calmness suffused me. It was as though the wind were singing to me, cradling me in its arms.

No sooner did I think this thought than two gigantic arms took form, then hands, shoulders, neck, and a face with shaggy eyebrows and puffed-up cheeks. "I am Zephyrus, the west wind god," he sang into my ear.

He held me securely. "We'll soon be there," he said as he started to descend.

He set me down in a green meadow and, as fast as he'd appeared, was gone.

The meadow was dotted with violets and

small yellow lilies. The air was balmy. A thrush sang in the distance: *kwee, kwee.* The song resounded again, then again, as though inviting me to follow.

I walked through the meadow. I crossed a stream into the woods. The thrush song led me to a clearing bathed in sunlight.

I closed my eyes against the glare. When I opened them again, a magical dwelling had sprung up. Ten golden columns supported the roof of ivory and citrus wood. The walls were sheeted with silver, embossed with figures of cavorting animals, both wild and tame. As I gazed in wonder, the silver portals opened wide.

I entered.

Everything shone with a golden brightness as though this dwelling had a sun all its own. I walked on jeweled floors through vast, magnificently furnished halls. Painted on the walls were fields with sheep, shepherds and shepherdesses, and forests with hunters and deer. On the ceiling danced the Graces, and the Muse Euterpe played her flute.

"Be happy here," said a voice behind me.

I turned around but saw no one.

"Everything within these walls is yours," the voice spoke on. Other voices, young girls' and women's, greeted me: "Welcome, Psyche."

"Where are you? *Who* are you?" I asked.

"We are your servants. Whatever you wish, we will provide, if we can."

"Let me see you," I asked of them. "Tell me your names."

"That we cannot," they answered. "We will serve you devotedly nevertheless."

They led me up a marble staircase and showed me a spacious chamber with an orchard of blossoming orange and almond trees painted on the walls. In the center stood a golden bed heaped high with pillows. Embroidered on the silken coverlet were red roses in full bloom.

I loosened my sandals. I suddenly felt weary from my journey and wanted to lie down.

"It is not yet time," lilted the voices.

They guided me to a dining hall and pointed to a couch shaped like a half-moon. Beside it stood a table set for a feast.

I reclined. Unseen hands placed delicious dishes before me, filled my goblet with Cyprian wine. An unseen choir sang. A lyre played as though of itself, more sweetly than any I had ever heard. Yet the melody declared itself merely the prelude to a music still to come.

When I was done feasting, I felt unseen hands take hold of mine. "We have prepared a bath for you." The servants led me there. They helped me undress. The water was soothing and fragrant. It washed my weariness away.

"Now the time approaches," murmured the servants, and they brought me to the bedchamber. A shimmering white, gossamer-fine gown lay on the bed. One pair of hands helped me put it on. Another brushed my hair. Others turned down the coverlet, fluffed the cushions. Still others drew the curtain.

"Now it is time. Lie down," said the voices.

No glimmer of moonlight or starlight shone in. I lay in utter darkness and became afraid. What if this magical dwelling were a sinister illusion, conjured up by the dragon bridegroom to lull me into complacency so that the horror would be all the greater when he took me into his power?

I started to imagine his fiery eyes, his nostrils breathing flames at me. But in my mind's ear the lyre now resumed its playing and the choir sang again, putting my fears to rest.

A breath blew out the flame of the little oil lamp on the bedside table.

"Now sleep," the servants' voices said. "We wish you joy of the night."

Their wish for me came true a thousandfold.

On my first morning in this magical place, kind though the unseen servants were, I came away to the meadow where Zephyrus had set me down. There, undisturbed, I could recall the first night and engrave each wondrous moment in my memory forever.

After sleeping awhile, I'd awakened in darkness, to a presence touching me on the lips, then on the eyes. My lips replied by opening; my eyes, by staying shut. I knew for certain it had to be so.

My father once had told me of an ancient belief that when the world was newly made, human beings were whole, each one female and male, united in one body. But when the world was older, a power envious of such bliss cleft human beings asunder. Ever since then, we humans must seek, and seldom find, our other part.

Mine had found me in the night. There was no mistaking him. My whole being welcomed him.

His presence awoke a thousand pleasures in my spirit, in my flesh. I could no more name them than name the myriad young shoots of grasses, buds and flowers, leafy plants that sprouted from the earth around me where I lay. Yet, as I recalled all the moments of the night, each pleasure reawakened and sang in me.

It was our bridal night.

The longer my eyes had remained closed, the more it seemed my fingertips received the power of vision, so well did they enable me to picture the perfection of my bridegroom's face and form.

We spoke a thousand endearments, exchanged a thousand caresses.

When the night was nearly over, he asked, "Can you be content not to behold me with your eyes? For that would spoil our happiness."

"Oh, yes," I replied, unhesitating. I promised I would never cast a light on him. And if ever he lingered past dawn, I would not look on him, even for the blink of an eye. Then we gave each other a thousand kisses to soften the sorrow when the moment of parting came.

My lips recalled them each by each, and I had no more fear. If his tender, gentle ways were mere illusion, if someday he revealed his true, his dragon form, then let me be a she-dragon, ready to join with him. I did not wish it otherwise. My only wish was for the time to pass quickly till night and my bridegroom returned.

IV

He never made the slightest sound, yet I always awoke, often from sweet dreams of him, the instant he entered our chamber.

Each night he awakened new joys in me. If he paused, I would whisper, "Love me in darkness," and he would resume ever more tenderly.

When he lay back, I would lean over him, push aside his hair, soft and curly to my fingers' touch, and begin to kiss him. I thought my lips were as free as his to wander and linger wherever they chose.

26

But once when I kissed him on his back, just below the shoulder, he startled and pulled away.

"Are you suddenly shy? Or is there something I must not feel? Dragons' prickly scales? Or dragons' wings, perhaps?" I called him "Dearest dragon," and I laughed.

I thought that he would laugh with me, as he always freely did. But he said, "Hush," and pressed his lips upon mine.

"Why must the hours of our nights speed by so fast?" I asked him once. "You make such wonders happen. Can you not hold back the hours?"

"I gladly would." His sadness matched my own that soon it would be dawn.

Always just before he left, I knew without his asking that he craved to hear my promise repeated. So I said it again and again: "To love you in darkness is all I want and need." And it eased our parting.

By day, when I was alone, my father's sorrowful face would sometimes pass before me like a cloud over my happiness.

My bridegroom knew, and asked me, "Are you grieving that your father thinks you dead and grieves for you?"

"Yes. And I wonder, do my sisters, too?"

"I heard in my travels that your sisters have come back to your father's kingdom," he said, taking me in his arms. "They mean to find out if the rumors of your death are true. As to their grieving, dearest Psyche, don't deceive yourself: your sisters feel no grief. Try to remember that tomorrow, when they climb to the mountain peak and shout your name out loud. Oh, Psyche, let them shout. Don't answer, if you prize the love we share."

"I prize it more than anything on earth. More than my life. But how can I not answer them if they have come so far to find me?"

"They mean you harm. They threaten our happiness together."

"No, surely not. You mustn't think unkindly of them."

He stroked my brow, then drew apart from me.

We lay in silence. I pictured Procne's and Petra's faces. I had not seen them for so long! I yearned, as I had in childhood, to be close to them. For once I wished the night away. And I wondered, How will I be able to stop myself from calling out their names?

My bridegroom turned to me and said, as though I had spoken my thoughts aloud, "Call to them if you must. I cannot forbid you what your heart requires. Bring them here. Make them welcome. Give them gifts, whatever they want."

"Thank you. You have lifted a weight of sadness from me. You won't regret it."

"We will see." He grasped me tight. The sadness he had taken from me was now upon him, and he said, "Don't believe them when they speak ill of me."

The next morning I ran to the meadow. Soon I heard their voices in the distance: "Psyche! Psyche!"

"Procne! Petra!" I all but flew through the woods and toward the mountain, shouting, "Dearest sisters, can you hear me?" I prayed to Zephyrus to carry my voice to their ears.

The wind god did better: he blew the clouds

apart and, revealing his giant form, came blustering toward me with my sisters clasped in his arms.

I bowed to him. "Great god, I thank you."

"Thank your husband. I do his bidding." He set them gently down and blew away.

They shivered from the cold through which they had been wafted, and from astonishment.

"Your husband commands the wind?" asked Procne, gasping for breath.

"How can that be?" asked Petra.

"How indeed?" I laughed. "Dearest sisters, all I know is that I'm so glad to see you!" I draped my shawl around their shoulders. I pulled them close. I smoothed their tousled hair. "This valley is always sunny. Soon you will be warm."

"You can't be half as glad as we are to find you still alive," said Procne.

"Imagine how dismayed we were to think you dead," said Petra.

I pulled them closer. They laid their cheeks against mine. A sweet contentment flowed over me. I felt encircled in their love.

They looked around. They saw the magic dwelling.

I led them to it.

The portals opened, and we went in. Their eyes grew wide.

"Compared to this, my husband's palace is a hovel," Procne said.

"My husband's, too," said Petra.

We walked along the jeweled floors through hall after splendid hall.

As we entered a smaller chamber, the doors of a wardrobe swung open, revealing lavish clothing.

"What marvelous magic is this?" they cried, delighted, and draped themselves in mantles, shawls, gowns. Mirrors appeared, and they preened.

On a table beside the wardrobe stood a box carved of ebony and sandalwood. Petra was the first to notice it. She approached, and it sprang open.

Then Procne saw it, too, and they both reached in, exclaiming, "What exquisite chrysolite earrings! And look at this fine onyx brooch!"

They put on the earrings and the brooch, then reached in for more. This time their hands collided, both grasping a ring of heavy gold with a blazing red stone in the center.

"I saw it first!" cried Procne.

"No, *I* did," Petra objected.

The casket lid came gently down. The next instant it opened again. Now there were two rings, exactly alike.

Overjoyed, my sisters put them on.

"Come, you must be hungry from your journey." I led them to the room with the table and couch in the shape of a half-moon. Now, when we entered, there were three such couches and tables.

"Recline. Be comfortable," I said.

Wine in golden goblets and delectable dishes appeared.

I thanked the unseen servants. I said, "These are my sisters, Procne and Petra. Will you welcome them?"

But the servants did not speak. And no lyre strummed; no chorus sang.

My sisters ate and drank their fill.

Procne said, "Oh, happy, lucky Psyche!"

Petra said, "How wonderful to be surrounded by such luxury! Tell us, dearest sister, who is your husband that he has all these riches and can command the wind?"

"Yes, tell us about him," said Procne. "How

did he obtain all this? Does he buy and sell goods all over the world? What goods? And does he own ships? How many? Where does he go when he is not here? When will he return?"

I smiled, shook my head, and said nothing.

"Is he young? Is he old? Is he dark? Is he fair? Is he corpulent or lean? Dull or entertaining?"

"Oh, better than 'entertaining.' Young, I would say but am not certain. Shapely. I can't tell you what color his hair is. It is always dark when we are together."

They tittered as they had long ago, discussing Procne's suitors.

"Dearest youngest sister, for whose sake we have journeyed such a distance," Procne said, "won't you at least tell us his name?"

"I can't."

"Why not?"

"I don't know it."

"But of course you do, you *must!*"

They raised their eyebrows and exchanged glances, and my sweet contentment ebbed.

"At least tell us what you call him when—" Petra embraced the air and puckered her lips. "Oh, *you* know when."

Procne said, her voice like honey, "Tell us, little sister."

I thought of the times they kept secrets from me, how bitter that had felt to me. And thinking, What harm could it do? I blurted, "Sometimes I call him my dragon."

They blinked and shuddered. "Then it's true!" they exclaimed. "Oh, we have come just in time. Poor, darling Psyche, don't be afraid—we can help you. We will save you!"

I laughed. "You don't understand! I am safe. I am happy. My bridegroom is the dearest, the kindest—"

"No, *you* don't understand," Procne said.

"Dear? Kind? How can you be so deceived?" asked Petra. "Have you not heard about the dragon who of late has been seen, but only by day, roaming about the countryside, stealing farmers' lambs, calves, piglets—"

"And babies, also, don't forget," Procne put in.

"Yes, and he eats them up alive!" said Petra. She looked at me in horror. "By night, he is your 'bridegroom.' Poor, simple Psyche, don't you see? He provides you with luxuries—"

"He feeds you delicacies," Procne went on. "He takes his joy of you in one way now—"

"But soon he will enjoy you in quite another way," said Petra.

"Devour you," said Procne.

They both pointed to my waist and said, "And the child in your belly, too."

My waist was as narrow as ever. But a cold dread gripped me around the heart, and a horror of my sisters. I leaped up from my couch and ran out through the corridors, out through the portals, not stopping to draw breath until I reached my meadow.

"Let them not follow me," I asked whatever god might be about.

But they soon found me there.

"Please hear us out," they asked in humble voices. "We did not mean to speak harshly. We only want to guard you from destruction. Just answer this one question: Does your husband forbid you to look on him?"

I nodded.

"That proves it. Psyche, you must save yourself. Listen, we will tell you how. Is there a lamp by your bedside?"

"Yes."

"Good. Make sure you have tinder to light it. Get hold of a knife. Make sure it is sharp—"

"Enough!" I put my fingers in my ears.

"Don't be childish," Petra said.

"We are your sisters—trust us," said Procne. "Wait till your husband is sound asleep. Then light the lamp and look. You must. It is your only hope.

"You will not see his true shape. He has the power to disguise himself, but not entirely. Look him over with great care. Somewhere on his body you will find evidence of his dragon nature—a talon in place of a toe, or a patch of scales perhaps.

"When you find it, plunge the knife into his throat. If you hesitate, he will sink his teeth into your flesh, devour you, hide and hair—"

"No more! May I never set eyes on you again, my sisters!"

My shout brought the wind god, invisible. He wrested their feet off the ground, whirled them up, and they were gone.

V

It ended. I lost my own, my all.

On a night soon after my sisters' visit, my bride-groom said, more tenderly than ever, "When first I saw you sitting in your father's garden, pulling petals off a daisy, I knew you had to be mine and loved you dearly. But now I love you as many times more as there are petals on all the daisies all over the wide earth."

I smiled and asked, "How so?"

"That day I saw only your beauty. Now I

know you, heart and soul. I have placed my trust in you. And here is another reason: before the year is out you will have our child."

I covered him with kisses. I cried aloud, "Oh, then I shall behold your features in the light of day!"

"And break your solemn promise?" he asked, alarmed.

"No, dearest, no. I only meant that I will look upon our child, who will resemble you, as children do their fathers."

"True," he replied, and was soothed.

All those nights, I'd felt there could be no greater happiness on earth than lying in my bridegroom's arms. But I was mistaken.

The next morning I awoke to sunshine streaming into the room, pouring light onto the painted fruit trees on the walls. As I looked around me, my whole being filled up with wonder at the new joy inside my heart. At first I could not name it. Then, yes, oh, yes, its name was Child—*our* child, in me!

From that moment on, everything around me was enhanced: our dwelling still more beautiful;

the servants even more attentive; the mealtime music more beguiling; each morsel of food, each sip of drink incomparably delectable.

When I was small, my old nurse used to tell me, "Carrying a child makes women weary all the time and only want to sleep," but not so, not me. I felt a heightened vigor, and where I had walked before, I ran, I skipped, I danced.

Often this new joy in me drove me outdoors to my meadow. And when I lay down, it was not for weariness. It was to breathe deeply into my body the scents of sorrel, clover, saxifrage, and of all other grasses and flowers in bloom; to take into my ears the coo of doves, the songs of thrushes, sparrows, larks; and to watch green lizards dart about, slide over narrow crevices in sunlit rocks nearby.

I lay in perfect peace, hands folded over my belly, and let nothing disturb me. My fears for my father had ceased. I felt as close to him as when I had lived inside his palace. I was sure he no longer mourned but knew, through the strong bond that had always linked us, how I flourished and thrived. As for Procne and Petra, I banished all thoughts of them.

Lying in the grass one morning, I glanced at the rocks and saw a dreadful sight there. Quickly I shut my eyes and prayed, "Juno and Lucina, goddesses who safeguard childbirth, take away what I saw."

I opened my eyes, and there it still was: the head of a very small lizard, mangled, bloody— spat out or left over by whatever fierce creature had devoured the rest of it.

A shouting started in my ears.

"You are troubled. Or are you ill? How can I comfort you?" asked my husband when he came to me that night.

I could not answer. I turned away, pretending to be exhausted. But I could not sleep for the clamorous shouting in my ears.

There are Furies in the world who fly about on wings of night and drive people mad. Perhaps this was their doing. But the words they screamed and the voices were my sisters': "Devour you, devour you, AND THE CHILD IN YOUR BELLY, TOO!"

Finally I did sleep, only to dream of a baby's

head, left bleeding, mangled, on a rock, and vultures circling overhead.

Next day—oh, would that it had been my last— I did not touch the morning meal of fresh-baked wheat bread, plums, and persimmons that my servants put before me. They offered to bring me other food, whatever I desired.

"Eat for the sake of the baby," said one.

"Do, for the baby," urged the others.

My heart pounded; my hands shook. But my voice was steady. "Thank you, good servants. Now do me another kindness: let me be. I long for solitude."

They did as I asked. None saw me take the sharp knife from the bread-slicing board and hide it in my bosom.

When I was small, after listening to my nurse's stories about robbers, pirates, and worse, I would wonder, How could evildoers bear forever knowing what they did?

I could not bear the weight on me of what that night I would have to do for the sake of the child inside me. I gave myself one hope, one chance at a way out.

It was this: to make him let me touch him on his back, just below his shoulders. If I felt no "patch of scales" or other trace of dragon nature there, the voices would stop importuning. I would melt into my husband's arms and let the dark suffuse us.

But on that night it was he who claimed exhaustion. He lay down on his back beside me and fell instantly asleep.

I lay awake. The darkness seemed thicker than ever before. I felt as though it were pressing upon my chest and would soon press on my belly, crushing the new little life inside.

"Light the lamp and look!" they clamored in my mind's ear.

I took the knife I had hidden under my pillow. I struck the tinder, lit the bedside lamp. And I looked.

Just as a trickle of rain cannot match the river Oceanus that flows around the earth, so human words cannot hope to describe what I beheld: boy, man, winged god in one—the son of Venus. This was my husband.

"Amor!" I exclaimed.

The knife fell from my hand. I burned so hot

with love for him, I thought I would burst into flames.

No, that was not my fate. My fate allowed me only moments to lose myself in his lustrous hair, noble forehead, tender ovals of his eyelids closed in sleep, his boyish cheeks; to feast my eyes on his lips that had given me pleasures untold; and memorize all the rest.

At the foot of the bed lay his bow and quiver of arrows.

How sharp were they? I touched one at the tip, and, being all a-tremble, let it nick my finger.

Then passion overwhelmed me. I could not do other than cover his body with mine.

The lamp shook in my hand. A drop of oil spilled from it onto his shoulder.

He startled up, cried out in pain, and pushed me aside. The bed, the walls, our very chamber crumbled into nothingness. He spread his snow-white, feathered wings. They beat the air. Without a word he flew into the sky.

But I had caught hold of his right leg and clung to it with greater strength than I had ever mustered. He swept through clouds, soared upward—I don't know how high or for how long.

Time lost its meaning. All I could grasp was the Now of clinging on.

When my strength began to fail, I prayed, "Let jagged rocks receive me and pierce my body through."

But I fell onto soft, sandy ground beside a river.

I looked up.

Amor stood atop a cypress tree and called down in a dreadful voice, "Psyche, it was for you that I defied my mother, disobeyed her. I was to avenge her by causing a passion in you for a lowly, worthless man. But your beauty so dazzled me that I allowed my own arrow to graze me. The rest you know: I trusted you. Now we are lost to each other."

His wings beat hard. He soared away. I watched until I could not see him anymore. Then I had no more need of eyes, for I wished never to look on any other sight in all the world but him.

VI ⚜

"Amor"—the name that Psyche gave him sang in the god's ear as he rose into the still-dark sky. All else in him despaired at leaving her behind.

Always before, he had flown as high and far as he pleased. But now the strength seemed to drain from him. Each wing beat was an effort. And he could not look ahead or up, nor take his eyes from Psyche lying huddled on the ground.

A flock of cranes flew by. In any other time, the god would have outsped them. Now his limbs felt heavy, threatening to pull him earthward.

New to him also was bodily pain: his shoulder

throbbing from the burn. Even stronger and more startling was the raw ache all through him of abandoning his beloved.

"What is happening to me?" he cried out.

He had risen high above the cypress tree. But his eyes were sharper than an eagle's eyes. He could still see Psyche.

As he watched her stagger toward the river near where she had fallen, a fear so great took hold of him that his wings missed beats and he faltered in his flight.

Psyche reached the riverbank, then slipped soundlessly into the waves.

The god saw, and he gasped. Air rushed into his lungs, and with it, the sharp, sudden knowledge of what humans feel when they breathe their last and cease to be. Everything inside him cried out, "Psyche must not die!" He summoned back what strength he could and commanded, "River, save her!"

The river cast her body onto dry land.

She did not move.

He could not tell if there was breath left in her, and he thought, "If she is dead, I will spend eternity longing to die, too."

The pain he felt throughout his being made him marvel at his old self, the one called Cupid, who for as far back as he could remember had blithely done his mother's bidding: caused desire to flare up in gods for gods, in gods for humans, in humans for one another, and had never worried what would come of it. Now face after face of those he had struck with his arrows appeared before his mind's eye. Some tore their cheeks with their fingernails. Some wept because their loves were at an end. And some, like his dear Psyche, sought to die.

He thought, Must love cause all this suffering?

Down on the ground, did Psyche stir? Or was it only that he wished it? Yes, slowly she rose to her feet. The god newly named Amor wept tears of relief. Had she been dead, his life would have been eternal anguish. This much he knew. All else in him was confusion.

Confusion . . . chaos . . . as in the time beyond imagining when only Chaos, Earth, and Sky, and I existed . . . not yet as my mother's son . . . not as Cupid, no . . . Eros was my name . . . I was a greater god. . . . What I did then was done at no one's bidding. . . .

Trying to remember back to the time when all things had begun made the earth tilt up at him, and he grew dizzy as though about to fall. Then suddenly his mother's face flashed before him. He winced from the pain in his shoulder and thought, She will heal me. I must fly to her.

VII 🎼

The god of the river refused me. Why take a wretched woman to his bosom whom a greater god has cast off? His waves did not submerge me but rather carried me to shore.

I lay down in the sand. Though drenched and nearly frozen, I resisted shivering, clenched my teeth, held myself rigid. I thought that the sorrow in my soul might turn to ice and I might die before night's darkness faded.

But no. The hour came when Amor used to part from me, though always to return at nightfall. Now he never would, for all the nights left of my life.

The edge of the eastern sky grew pale, soft violet, then pink, then gold. From childhood on, I'd loved this wondrous bright promise of ever-new beginnings. But what use were beginnings to me, now that *my* promise was broken?

I turned to the west, where all was darkness.

From that direction came a song, cheerful as a field of buttercups. First I heard just one deep, zestful voice. Then a second, high and sweet, joined in.

As the dawn advanced and darkness yielded, I discerned a shape—no, two shapes—seated in the meadow that sloped up from the riverbank: a manlike goat—no, goatlike man—his arm around a girl? A woman?

It was the nymph named Echo, for no sooner did I think I saw her than she was gone, and only the sound of her singing lingered.

When the sky grew lighter, I saw that the goat-man's legs were covered with wavy white and brown fur. His body was muscular and smooth; his face both old and young. For hair he had wild, shaggy curls. From his forehead sprouted goat's horns.

He patted the ground beside him. "Come sit here with me. Don't be afraid."

His voice was so inviting, his manner so kindly, that I could not refuse.

When I was seated beside him, he wagged a furry finger in my face and said, "To seek to die before your time is folly. You won, and lost, the great god Love. But who is to say you cannot win him back? Keep your heart open. Find him. And, beautiful young Psyche, let me tell you— it's a lucky thing to meet up with a crusty old goat-man like me."

His yellow-green eyes flashed fire into mine. Laughter so compelling burst from deep down in his throat, that I, who'd thought I'd never laugh again, laughed right along.

He touched me gently on the cheek and said, "You know me."

Yes. He was Pan.

He gave a goatherd's call. A brown-flecked she-goat came trotting down the meadow and stood before him, her udders so full that drops of milk dripped to the ground.

He milked her into his hand, then put his hand to my lips, and I drank.

I knew not whether it was the song, or Pan's

words, or the warm, frothy milk, or all of those together that gave me new hope and strength.

"Thank you for your kindness," I said—to the she-goat, for Pan had vanished.

She pointed her horns to the path along the river.

So that was the path I took.

At noon I came to a road branching off from the river. The signpost told me that this road led to my sister Procne's kingdom.

Which road should I follow? While I stood there wondering, my sister Procne's lies resounded in my head. Her face came into my mind's eye, feigning fondness, feigning worry, all the while concealing hatred and the harm she meant to do. As I recalled these things, a throbbing began in my head, in the hollow place behind my right ear. I pressed my finger to it, but it would not stop.

"That is the place where vengeance sits," my old nurse used to say. I had not believed her. But suddenly I knew which road I had to take.

Toward evening I arrived in the capital of my sister Procne's kingdom.

51

I went to the palace.

Procne welcomed me and asked me sweetly, "Oh, poor Psyche, what has happened to you?"

I held myself taut in her embrace.

I said, "I did as you advised. I lit the lamp and shone it on my husband. A drop of oil spilled and burned him on the shoulder. He spread his wings, flew away—"

"Were they dragon's wings?" she asked.

"No, Procne. They were a god's wings—"

"A god? What god?" Her face contorted. It became a battleground for disbelief struggling with something vile that I now recognized as her monstrous envy of me.

"It was Venus's son. It was Amor, none other." And I asked her, with the throbbing growing louder, "Shall I tell you what he said before he left me?"

"Yes, yes, tell me, quickly!"

She was my sister, once dear to me. But she had lied, wishing me to lose all that I had. These truths warred within me. The second outweighed the first. Besides, the throbbing in my head now felt like hammer blows, and it made me tell her, "Amor said, 'I will find a woman who is worthy of me and marry her instead.' "

"Oh, did he really say that?" Procne asked, wild excitement in her voice.

I looked into her eyes and saw, as clearly as though it were happening then and there, what Procne planned to do.

She invited me to stay, but I refused. I had farther to travel. The throbbing drove me on.

After three days I came to Petra's realm, and I went straight to the palace.

Petra asked, ever so sweetly, "Poor Psyche, all ragged and barefoot, what has happened to you?"

I answered her as I had answered Procne and foresaw as well what she would do.

"Stay—you are welcome here," she urged. "Let me care for you."

"No." I took leave of her. My voice, my manner were tranquil and composed. But the throbbing throbbed on with a fierceness that spread all through me. I knew it would continue till my vengeance was complete.

*   *   *

Many nights later, I found shelter in an abandoned hut just before a storm broke. I was tired and fell fitfully asleep.

When I awoke, the broken shutters were banging, the flimsy walls creaking and groaning. The storm raged all around.

The door blew open. The storm burst in and took shape: it was Zephyrus. Then all grew calm as he took me in his arms and sang into my ear: "Hear what became of your sisters. Procne, in her envy, thought *she* deserved a god for her husband. She left the husband she already had and traveled back to your father's kingdom, back to the rocky peak. There she stood and shouted, 'Amor, here I come, a woman worthy of you! Wind, carry me to the magic dwelling!' She took a headlong leap, plunged onto rocks that pierced her flesh, and died.

"Three days later, your sister Petra, envying you no less, climbed to the rocky peak and met with the same fate."

Then Zephyrus blew out the door, leaving behind the calm that he had brought.

I did not feel remorse for setting Procne and

Petra's fate in motion. Oh, but I grieved from the depth of my heart and wept for the sisters I had wished them to be. Then the throbbing ceased. I lay down and slept deeply.

VIII

Venus, basking in the cradle-like valley between two waves, flicking salt water idly from her beringed fingers, felt perfectly at peace. For she was certain that her son had done his duty and punished her upstart rival.

She tipped her head backward, looked up, and saw a white gull flying down.

The gull alighted on the crest of the nearer wave. He bowed his head low and screeched respectfully, "Great Venus, don't be angry with me for bringing you distressing news—"

"What news?" she asked impatiently.

"*Your son has suffered an injury. He fled to your dwelling and lies in pain on your bed. And, and—*" The gull fluttered his wings in agitation.

"*And what? Out with it,*" growled the goddess.

"*People are saying it was his lover, a mere human creature, who inflicted the harm.*"

"*His lover? What 'mere human creature'?*"

"*A princess—*"

"*Her name?*"

"*Psyche,*" screeched the gull, then took flight in alarm, for Venus flailed her arms and thrashed the water, causing it to spurt up in great spumes.

"*My own son—oh, what dishonor! By joining with that impudent 'new Venus,' he rebels against my rule, challenges my authority, my very divinity! Was ever a goddess more humiliated and betrayed?*"

Then, too, there was his injury. For all that he had ceased to behave like a son to her, she was still his mother, and it worried her.

Thinking, *I must go to him,* she willed herself up from the sea, through the sky, and past the gate of clouds to the lofty heights of Mount Olympus.

Her son was not in her palace there.

Venus cursed the gull for not telling to which of her dwellings Cupid had fled.

I'll hurry down to earth, but in a style befitting my godhood, she decided. She went to the gods' carriage yard. There stood the chariot that her onetime husband, the smith-god Vulcan, had crafted for her. It was of burnished gold, embellished all over with intricate filigree. No sooner did she mount to the driver's seat than four white doves came flying. They offered their iridescent necks to the jeweled harness and drew her toward earth.

Along the way she met the messenger-god Mercury and greeted him, "Hail, brother from Arcadia," for that was the place of his birth.

He flew on winged sandals alongside her chariot while she poured out her story to him. "I feel torn in two," she confided, looking to him for sympathy, for they were fond of each other and had once been lovers. "My wrath impels me to search for that wretched Psyche and teach her lessons she won't soon forget. But I cannot take the time. Cupid needs me. After all, he's still my son, and injured. I must take care of him. Mercury, dear brother-god, will you find Psyche and bring her to me so that justice may be done?"

Mercury flew close, and laid his hand on her hair. "Be calm, fair sister from the sea. Go to Cupid. I will look for Psyche."

* * *

When Venus reached her favorite earthly dwelling, she found her son lying stretched out on her bed.

"Where is your wound? Let me see it," she demanded.

"Here, on my shoulder, Mother."

She applied salves and lotions. But all the while she soothed the burn, she rebuked him: "My injury is worse by far, and you inflicted it on me. Of all the earthly women you might have chosen to dally with, you chose the one I hate the most—"

"It was no 'dalliance,' Mother—"

"Don't talk. Talk will make you weaker." She went on rebuking him: "I asked you to inflame the girl's heart with a passion for the crudest, meanest fool, remember?" Venus gave a bitter laugh. "You are that fool. And, worse, a traitorous son. By joining with my rival, you thought to steal away my power."

"Mother, Psyche never wished to be your rival—"

"Obey me and be silent. Defy me again, and I promise you I will give your bow and arrows to the lowliest slave in my employ to put to better use than you. Now move closer, and hold still."

She applied a hot poultice to the burn. It stung. He winced and moaned.

His pain touched her. She pulled the poultice away. She smoothed his curls; she stroked his neck, put her lips to the burn. "There, is that better?"

He murmured yes.

"Good. Now I'll leave you. Sleep will restore you, my Cupid."

Hearing her call him by the old name drained him of more strength. He felt small. He turned on his side, bent his knees, and curled up. His limbs and eyelids grew heavy. Just for a moment, before sleep overcame him, he wondered, Was I really the god my beloved called Amor? Or did I dream all that?

Meantime his mother had gone out, locking the door behind her. She strode down a tree-shaded promenade through her orchards and gardens and looked up, hoping to see the gleam of silver-winged sandals.

She knit her eyebrows together, planning dire punishments for the girl who had caused her all this woe, and, raising her fist to the sky, she shouted, "Mercury, don't tarry! Bring Psyche to me now!"

IX ⚭

The morning after Zephyrus had sung to me of my sisters, I awoke to sunshine and birdsong. The storm had cleansed woods, fields, and meadows, and made their greenness sparkle. I, too, felt cleansed as I set out afresh, resolved to find my love.

Stopping at crossroads, praying to Mercury to guide my steps, for he was god of travelers, I searched and searched through weeks and months and through many kingdoms.

Dandelion leaves, wild fruits, and berries sustained me—mushrooms also, for when I was little my nurse had taught me how to tell which were good and which were poisonous. When I was thirsty, I drank from clear-flowing streams; when weary, I slept wherever I found shelter.

Late one day I saw a temple on a hilltop. For no better reason than that the setting sun made the temple's columns glow, I thought, Perhaps— who can say?—I will find Amor there.

I climbed up and went in. Gifts of cornstalks, ears of barley, scythes, and sickles told me whose temple this was. But they'd been flung about in disorder, as though by harvesters after a long day's work.

"Ceres, bountiful goddess of the earth," I prayed, "you searched far and wide for your daughter Proserpina when the god of the Underworld stole her away. You know how it is to search the world over for someone you have lost. I have lost my love, my Amor. Help me find him!"

To lend weight to my prayer, I started to arrange the offerings in their proper order.

Suddenly the goddess stood before me, mysterious and motherly, stalks of corn and purple asters in her darkly flowing hair.

"You do well to tend my altar. But you had

better flee, for Venus is angry with you. She commanded our brother-god Mercury to seek you out and deliver you to her."

That Venus was angry I knew. But the thought that Mercury, whose guidance I had counted on, was against me, too, filled me with dread.

I threw myself at Ceres's feet and begged her, "Let me hide in your temple till Venus's anger abates."

"That will not happen on its own," replied the goddess.

"What do you mean? What must I do?"

"I cannot tell you. But I wish you well." She touched me on the forehead and sent me away.

I came to another temple. This one stood in a valley, surrounded by poplar trees. From the doorposts hung a cloak of peacock feathers.

I went in and prayed to Juno, whose sacred bird the peacock was, "Mighty queen of the gods, sister and wife of Jupiter, protector of marriages, help me find my husband and shield me from Venus's anger."

Juno appeared in regal splendor, crowned

with a jeweled diadem, holding a golden scepter, and spoke: "I do indeed protect marriages, but of equals. I do not recognize as 'marriage' the coupling of a god with a mortal such as you. I've endured enough such wantonness from my faithless husband. No, I will not shield you from Venus. Leave my sanctuary. Go!" She brandished her scepter at me.

I ran till I was breathless. I feared she would come after me and punish me herself.

That night I huddled in a corner of a burned-out farmhouse, hungry, thirsty, tired, but too afraid to sleep. And I questioned, with Venus, Mercury, and Juno against me, was it madness to go on?

In the morning, while washing myself at a spring, I heard a whir of wings above the trees and grew terrified. I hid my face behind my hands, so certain was I that it was Mercury come to snatch me up.

But it was only a woodland falcon searching for his morning meal, some hapless little mouse or mole hiding in the grass.

Cowering and trembling, I felt a kinship with such small and helpless creatures.

Then still another fear took hold of me: could I no longer distinguish past from present? For I beheld a sight that I had seen before: a she-goat trotting toward me, brown-flecked, udders round and full. Was it an apparition that would disappear the instant I reached out?

The goat came close, stood still, looked at me with yellow eyes, and let me milk her.

When I had drunk the milk, my courage returned. I would no longer cringe in fright at every rustling noise and shadow on the ground. I knew now what I had to do: go of my own accord to Venus. Swear that I had always honored her, had never knowingly done anything to offend her. And if that was to no avail, I would submit myself to her wrath.

I started out at once, trusting my own feet to guide me right. I walked tirelessly on. A hope sustained me that by finding Venus, I might find my love as well.

After a day and a night, the path I followed widened and became a tree-shaded promenade. On either side were orchards and gardens. In the distance rose a stately dwelling. As I neared it, I saw a woman approaching—no, a goddess. It was she. I knew her by the radiant beauty that also graced my husband's form and face.

Eyes cast down, I ran to her, stooped to the ground, and touched my lips to the hem of her gown.

"Mother of my love, I come willingly into your presence."

She pulled the hem of her gown away. She called me "Murderess!"

Amor, dead? Everything turned dark before my eyes. The fingernails of my right hand, with which I'd held the knife, dug deep into the flesh of my palm. My left hand clenched into a fist as though around the lamp I'd held. My feet lost their hold as though the ground beneath them trembled. If I was a murderess, then even gods could die, for I had killed my love. . . .

Venus pulled me up by the hair. The pain of it returned me to my senses.

"Goddess, I swear to you by all that is sacred, I did not murder your son. I wounded him, yes, to my everlasting sorrow. But the gods are immortal, are they not? Gods cannot die—is that not true? So tell me, I beg you, in what way am

I—" My tongue grew thick, I could not utter the word.

"Murderess," she said again. "You *wanted* to kill him."

"No! I feared he was a dragon, had been told so. Once I beheld my husband, I wanted only to love him with every breath I drew, with my whole heart and soul forever, believe me!"

"Nobly spoken," Venus said, "but no more true than that word 'husband.' You are no more married to my son than a mongrel bitch is married to the father of her latest litter. As for your coming willingly into my presence, that shall not lighten your punishment by one jot."

She called her servants. "Go to the granary. Fill up seven sacks of seeds and grains, and bring them here."

They did so and spilled out the contents— wheat, barley, millet, lentils, beans, poppy seeds, and vetch seeds.

"Now mix them all together."

The servants did, then piled them into a heap that stood taller than I.

"Soon you will labor to bring forth the child you carry—*if* I allow it," Venus threatened.

"First you must labor for me, and this is how you shall begin: sort the seven kinds of grains and seeds into seven separate heaps, each of its own kind only. Finish before nightfall, or you will regret it." And she strode away.

Already the sun stood low. I thought the heap contained no fewer grains and seeds than a cloudless night sky has stars.

I knelt down and started sorting, futile though it seemed. I told myself, though I could not make myself believe it, that when Venus returned and saw me hard at work, she might relent.

Gray, white, brown, black, white, gray. . . . Round, oval, small, smaller, dotlike, almost too small to grasp. . . . I sorted and sorted till my fingers ached and my eyes were bleary.

One dark little grain stuck to my finger. No, not a grain, for it had legs. It scrabbled onto my fingertip, and I saw what it was: an ant, the country kind.

It leaped off to the ground.

"Sisters, come!" it called. "Busy children of generous Earth, we must help Psyche, quickly! She is the wife of Love himself, and in grave danger!"

Then from a furrow in the ground came wave

upon wave of six-legged ants, vast armies of them, not many fewer than there were grains and seeds. They set to work at once, using one pair of legs to stand on and two pairs of legs for sorting. Soon the tremendous heap was gone. In its place stood seven piles, neatly stacked—one each of wheat, barley, millet, lentils, beans, poppy, and vetch.

At sundown Venus returned.

"You are a witch!" she raged. "First you bewitched my son, and now you have ensnared some unknown power to do your work for you."

She threw me a crust of bread. "Go spend the night in the henhouse. Practice your witchcraft on the hens. You will need it for your further labors."

X 🌸

The henhouse was evil smelling, and the hens clucked noisily in their sleep. It was as squalid a resting place as the bedchamber I had shared with Amor was sumptuous. All the same, I rested well, for I felt nearer to Amor than on any night since losing him.

In the morning I washed myself at a wooden trough outside the henhouse. A slave who came to collect the eggs lent me her crude comb.

I was struggling to free my hair of knots and tangles when suddenly the goddess stood before me. Her radiance was dazzling. I shielded my eyes with my hand.

But she pushed my hand away and laughed. "To think they called *you* 'the new Venus'!" She loosened her hair, let its lustrous waves cascade down to her hips, and commanded, "Look at me. Behold the goddess you dared to rival."

I dropped to my knees. "Believe me—that was never my intent."

"Intent or no, you stole my worshipers from me, and, as if that were not enough, you stole my wayward son as well. Stand up now. Pay attention. I will tell you your next task.

"Go to the end of my orchards and gardens. You will come to a stream. Wade across. On the far bank is a grove. In that grove roam seven shining golden sheep. Fetch me seven strands of their precious wool, one strand from each sheep."

I bowed to her and started out.

When I came to the stream and looked across, all I saw of sheep were distant golden flashes in dense underbrush.

I waded into the water.

When I had crossed halfway, a voice from the other bank called, "Psyche, wait!"

Where had I heard that voice before? I looked all around but saw no one. So I waded on.

"Don't come nearer," the voice warned.

"Who are you? Show yourself!" I called.

The air was calm. No breeze was blowing. The reeds on the bank stood motionless—all but one green tall one. That reed swayed rhythmically to and fro.

"I am the reed Pan uses when he makes his pipes," it called. "He lent me his voice. And I tell you, turn back. Don't set foot on this bank."

"But I must! Venus commanded me to fetch her some wool from the seven golden sheep in the grove—"

At that moment a roaring began. It was as unlike the bleating of sheep as is thunder unlike the cry of a child. A golden monster came into view. It was shaped like a sheep but three times as large, with horns like daggers and eyes as bloodshot as those of a maddened bull.

"Don't be afraid," Pan's reed said. "You are safe. The sheep will not enter the water."

"But what am I to do?"

"Go back to the bank. Sit under the tall plane tree over there, and wait. These sheep borrow heat from the blazing sun. It puts them in a frenzy, and they kill any humans who venture near. They gore them with their sharp horns, butt them to death with their stony foreheads, or bite them with their poisonous teeth. But I'll tell you a secret. Listen: in the cool of late afternoon, they lie down, lulled by the murmur of the stream, and fall asleep."

I went back and I waited. In late afternoon, just as the reed had predicted, the seven sheep lay down in the grove and soon were snoring loudly.

Then I crossed the stream, stopping at the shore to kiss the reed for thanks.

The sheep's wool ranged from pale to deepest gold. Plentiful clumps of it hung from twigs and branches. As quickly as I could, I plucked seven strands, one to match each sheep's color.

On my way back to Venus's domain, the strands of wool glowed in my hands, as richly hued as the setting sun. I allowed myself to fancy Venus receiving them with pleasure.

"Witch!" she cried, snatching the strands from me.

The next morning she gave me my third labor.

"Do you see the tall, steep mountain in the

distant north? That is Mount Aroanius. A dark river cascades down its craggy slope into a gorge below, then floods the Stygian marshes and feeds the River of Wailing. Fetch me water from the gorge." She handed me a jar of polished crystal. "Fill this jar to the brim. And don't try to deceive me by taking water from some place other than the very center of the gorge."

She sent me on my way.

I wished it were the mountain in my father's kingdom. Oh, that my father were by my side, and that the time with my love were still to come!

The path up Mount Aroanius led to a cliff as slippery as glass and as steep as a wall. From this cliff and into the gorge below burst the roiling waters of the Styx. Around the gorge slithered giant serpents, all intertwined, more than I could count. They stretched their necks out, bared their fangs, flicked their forked tongues, and never blinked their fiery eyes as they guarded the sacred water.

"Be off! Be off! Or death!" the water sang.

I stood still as a stone. The slightest motion would have lost me my foothold. There was nothing to hold on to, no branch, nor any rock to break my fall straight down into the gorge.

Pan's words echoed in my ears: "To seek to die before your time is folly." But it was plain that now my time had come.

"Mercury, come find me now," I prayed. "I went to Venus on my own—no need to bring me there. Conduct me to the Underworld, as you do other mortals, but by a gentler way than plunging into this abyss."

Not Mercury, but a huge eagle, came flying down on wings as wide as sails and hung in the air, obscuring the sky. "Poor, frail human creature," he screamed, "do you not know that even the gods, and even my master, mighty Jupiter, fear the waters of the Styx?"

"I fear them, too!" And feared this eagle no less, who with a flick of his wing could send me hurtling down.

"Wife of Cupid," he screamed, but not so shrilly, "I owe your husband a favor. He helped me bring Prince Ganymede up to Heaven to be Jupiter's cupbearer. In return for that, I will help you now."

He took the crystal jar from me. Clasping it in his sharp talons, he shot down to the gorge.

"Be off! Be off! Or death!" the torrent roared as he flew by with dazzling speed.

The serpents lashed themselves about, darting their heads this way and that, flicking their tongues, and hissing their fury at how deftly this intruder from on high avoided their cruel fangs.

He zigzagged to the center, trailed the jar in the water, and with lightning speed brought it back to me.

"Eagle of Jupiter, thank you," I called as he winged away, up through thick, dark clouds.

XI

Climbing down Mount Aroanius, I felt the child weigh heavy in my belly. I could not tell how long it was since I'd set out on this third task. But the leaves of many trees had turned from green to red and brown. Other trees stood bare.

In Venus's orchards, the fruit had all been harvested. Summer was at an end.

Venus came toward me, astonished to see me return.

I placed the crystal jar in her hands. It was full

to the brim; not a drop had spilled. I hardly dared hope for words of thanks or praise from her.

She gazed into the water's depth, then dipped her finger in and dabbed wetness on her eyelids.

"Come, Psyche." She took me by the hand. "You shall not sleep in the henhouse tonight."

She led me into her dwelling, to a dining hall. Slaves brought me a supper of fresh bread, meats, and wine. "Eat, drink," Venus urged. "Make yourself strong for tomorrow."

Then she showed me to a guest chamber and wished me a restful night.

I was tired, and glad to have the comfort of a proper bed. But wondering what the next day would bring kept me awake a long time.

When at last I slept, I fell into a dream of the serpents from the gorge. "The Styx, the Styx," they hissed, and coiled themselves around me.

My own voice shouting, "Amor! Amor!" woke me. My heart beat fast. I sensed that he was near. I held my breath and waited.

But he did not come.

A bleak, vast loneliness descended on me. I felt as though I were the only living human creature anywhere on earth.

* * *

Early next morning, Venus came in, still wearing her nightgown, with her hair flowing loose around her. She said, "Your safe return from the Stygian gorge tells me that the powers who protect you are greater than I. I hope therefore that you can help me. Are you willing?"

"Help you? How?" I asked.

"I have been greatly troubled of late," she said, as though confiding in me. "I fear that my much-vaunted beauty has begun to fade. Psyche, will you help me to restore it?"

"Your beauty is immutable," I said, not daring to look her full in the face.

"Human vision is dim. You cannot judge. I ask you again, will you help me?"

"Yes, if I can. What would you have me do?"

She brought forth an object from the folds of her gown. It was a small round box carved of ivory with a border of crocuses engraved on the lid. She said, "Take this to Queen Proserpina. Ask her to lend me a little of her beauty."

An icy chill went through me. "But autumn has come. Proserpina has gone to Tartarus, deep down in the Underworld. And no one can come back from there," I said with quaking voice.

"You are mistaken," Venus answered. "Proserpina returns each year, bringing spring back with her. And the singer Orpheus returned, although he failed to bring Eurydice back with him."

"But Orpheus had Apollo for a father. Proserpina is herself a goddess. I am mortal."

"A fact you forgot when you ensnared a god to be your lover," Venus said, her bitter tone returning.

"I never forgot my parentage. Nor did I 'ensnare'—"

"Do not speak of it to me. Pray to the powers who helped you before that they help you again.

"Here, take these, lest it be said that I did nothing to protect you." She gave me two coins and two pieces of barley bread soaked in honey.

"What must I do with them?"

"Secret things. Depart at once. Head west. I cannot tell you more."

XII ⚜

Amor, all this time, lay oblivious in his mother's bed, dreaming the days and nights away.

In one dream—it seemed so real!—he and Psyche were happily together in the magic palace. But suddenly she turned into a slave. He saw her kneel before a cruel mistress whom he well knew but could not name. He tried with all his might to shout, "Psyche, stand up! Be free! Be mine!" But no sound came from his lips.

In other dreams, bloodthirsty beasts pursued her. But when he tried to fly to her defense, his wings were leaden and could not beat.

One midnight, he heard her anguished voice cry,

"Amor! Amor!" Again it seemed so real! He went to find her. But then he awoke, still in his mother's bed, and it was morning.

Now, for the first time since taking refuge here, he sat upright. And he reeled, not from the effort, but from the sharp, stabbing pang of knowing that Psyche was gone.

"Mother, Mother!" he called out.

Venus came.

"Psyche was here—I know it. You kept her from me. Don't deny it! And now she is gone. Tell me where!"

"Cupid, be quiet. You are raving!" Venus felt his forehead, then blew on her fingers, "Whhh," as though they had touched fire. "Consorting with a human has made you prone to human afflictions. You are feverish, delirious. Calm yourself." She prevailed on him to lie down again.

"Good. Now Mother will sit beside you." She played with a lock of his hair, winding it like silken threads around her finger. She smoothed fresh salve onto his shoulder. She placed a cool compress on his head. "There, is that not better?" She gave him motherly kisses. "Close your eyes now. Go to sleep. And soon you'll be yourself again, my own sweet boy, my Cupid."

He half closed his eyes.

She tiptoed to the door.

But he was still awake and asked, "To what place did you send Psyche?"

"Hush—be quiet. Banish Psyche from your thoughts—"

"Never!" He threw off the compress, and the coverlet, too. "You sent her somewhere dreadful—I can feel it. Mother, if she is lost to me because of you, you will lose my love forever. I ask for the last time: Where is Psyche?"

"Nowhere that you can follow," Venus said, and went out, locking the lock behind her.

The god sprang to his feet. An ungodlike feeling, shame, assailed him. He beat his fists against his chest for having lain in lassitude and helplessness so long.

"I will be myself again," he resolved, "not Venus's obedient Cupid, but Eros and Amor in one!"

All his strength returned.

One leap, and he was at the door. One touch, and the lock sprang open. Out he flew on supple wings, leaving his mother's domain behind, and swore he would not rest until he found his love.

* * *

He flew over many lands. Often he descended, and, disguised as a wayfarer, asked in towns and villages if anyone had seen her.

One day he flew through a blanket of clouds and came upon Mercury, leaping nimbly over their arched backs.

"Cupid, well met," called the messenger-god. "I bring you word from Jupiter. He commands your presence at tomorrow's council on Mount Olympus. And I warn you, Brother, he is vexed with you already for staying too long absent from Olympus."

"I cannot come," Amor replied.

"Do you mean to vex him more?"

"I cannot do otherwise. Oh, Mercury, first I must find my love. You are the god who watches over travelers. Tell me, have you seen her?"

"Yes." Mercury named all the places where Psyche had been. He told of the hardships she had endured and of the first three tasks she carried out for Venus.

Amor listened, grief-struck. "Where is she now?" he asked.

"Somewhere you cannot follow."

"That is what my mother said. Do you side with Venus in this? Are you against me?"

"*I take no sides,*" *said Mercury.*

"*I'll follow Psyche to any place on earth!*" *Amor declared.*

Then he read the silence in Mercury's eyes, and understood: "The place my mother sent her is nowhere on the earth. And Jupiter forbids us gods to go there, except you. Oh, Mercury, why did you not go with her and watch over her?"

"*It is forbidden to me also, except when I guide the souls of the dead,*" *Mercury replied.*

"*Forbidden or not, I'll go to her!*" *Amor cried out.*

"*Jupiter metes out harsh punishments,*" *Mercury cautioned. "Remember Prometheus, whom he chained to a rock—*"

Amor closed his ears to this. "Tell me the way," *he said.*

With grave reluctance, Mercury complied.

Amor flew off at once.

Mercury flew down to Venus. He found her agitated, ordering her slaves about.

"*Bring my combs, my golden hair clips. Not those, the others. No, don't put them there! Go away. I'll do it myself.*" *She combed her hair this way and that.*

She threw a comb at the wall. She slumped in her chair, let her head droop forward, scooped her hair up from the nape of her neck and sent it falling over her face.

Mercury parted her hair like a curtain and looked at her fondly. "Dear Venus, Jupiter bids you come to the gods' council on Olympus tomorrow. But better still, come with me now. He has missed you terribly and will be glad to see you sooner."

"Not like this. Don't you see how disheveled and worn I look?"

"I see how lovely you are—and how mistaken for thinking it not so. Come, lend me your company. We can journey in your chariot, if you like."

"No. I will wait here for Psyche, and for news of my son, who has escaped from my care."

"Then you may wait forever. I must return to Olympus. I hope you will follow me as Jupiter requires." Mercury bent to strap one sandal more tightly around his leg. "Sister, farewell." And he departed.

Venus went back to her dressing table. She took up her mirror and gasped.

A pair of eyes looked darkly back—Cupid's eyes, accusing her, or so it seemed to the goddess. "If Psyche is lost to me because of you, you will lose my love forever," Venus heard him say as clearly as if he were standing at her side.

She put down the mirror. She laid her head on her arms and moaned, "What have I done?"

XIII ⌘

I walked westward for an hour or so. Then I came
to a crossroads with a signpost that had the head of
Mercury on it. His eyes, though carved of wood,
looked on me kindly.

I thanked him that he did not take me forcibly
to Venus. And I prayed, "Conductor of souls to
the Underworld, help me in my ignorance and
need. Show me the way to Tartarus."

The left-hand marker of the signpost creaked
and shook.

The god head's wooden lips stayed shut. Yet
a voice distinctly told me, "Go to the peninsula

of Taenarus. There you will see a wide, round crater. It leads down to the world below. Hurl yourself in. Follow the road before you. Be brave and pitiless. Speak to no one along the way.''

"What must I do with the coins and barley bread that Venus gave to me?''

"When you reach the river, give one coin to the ferryman. But say not a word to him, nor to anyone along the shore when you reach the other side.

"The three-headed watchdog Cerberus guards the entrance to the palace of the dead. Look him bravely in all six eyes, and throw him one piece of honey-soaked barley bread for a sop.

"Once inside the palace, refuse to sit anywhere but on the floor. Refuse all delicacies. Ask only for a slice of common bread. . . .'' The voice grew faint.

"Great Mercury, do not withdraw your presence yet! Tell me, how can I return?''

"By the sop, by the coin, and forbearance. Do not open the box,'' warned the voice, and spoke no more.

I went to the peninsula of Taenarus. I leaped into the crater and hurtled down into a world neither light nor dark, but shrouded in impenetrable gloom.

A road stretched before me. I followed it. Phantom shapes both animal and human arose to my right, to my left. They muttered, moaned, and disappeared.

A lame ass and lame driver came hobbling toward me. The ass bore a load of wooden branches, lashed to its back. The rope broke. The branches fell to the ground.

"Please, oh, please," begged the driver, "hand me the rope so I can tie up the load again."

Pity wrenched me. But I did not stop, or speak, or help. When I glanced back, ass and driver had vanished.

Down in that realm, there is no way to measure time. However long it took me, at last I came to the dreaded River of Wailing, also known as Styx.

Along the shore stood a throng of shadowy figures. They were the hapless dead who'd brought no coins. "Charon, good ferryman, take us across!" they pleaded in spectral voices—in vain, doomed to roam the nearer bank forever.

I hardened my heart and pushed my way through. The ruffian Charon, clothed in rags, held out a filthy hand, into which I dropped one coin. His fingers closed around it, and he motioned me aboard.

The river was rank and sluggish. An old man's corpse came floating by, raising a skeleton arm, imploring, "Haul me up!"

I closed my ears to his cries.

The farther shore was enveloped in a gloom as thick as storm clouds forever on the verge of breaking. Disembarking, I saw three insubstantial shapes of women at a loom. "Help us weave our cloth!" they wailed.

I averted my eyes and hurried past.

Dark walls towered in the distance. Coming nearer, I heard a bone-chilling clamor.

The nearer I came, the louder it grew.

It was the giant hound Cerberus, guarding the palace of the dead. The eyes in each of his three heads blazed fire, and all his nostrils flared. When he opened wide his three cruel maws, he bared six rows of sharpest teeth, and growled and barked and howled from deep down in all three gullets.

I threw one sop his way. He caught it in his middle maw, and no sooner swallowed than he collapsed in a stupor.

Now nothing barred my way.

I crossed the threshold and entered a reception hall. Along the walls stood rows of tall lamps, but they gave only an eerie light.

Queen Proserpina herself came to greet me. Her earth-brown eyes resembled those of her mother, Ceres. But her face was deathly pale and her manner deeply sad.

"You must be tired. Won't you sit here?" She offered me a luxuriantly cushioned chair.

Exhausted, I longed to sit there but said, "Forgive me, I must not," and instead sat down on the floor.

Servants came with trays of appetizing meats, ripe, sweet-smelling fruits, and a goblet of dark red wine.

I was hungry and thirsty. But, to Proserpina's chagrin, I ate only a slice of common bread.

"Did you bring me something?" she asked.

I held out the box. "Will you put in a touch of your beauty for the goddess Venus?"

"*My* 'beauty,' wan and pale, for Venus? When she is mistress over all of earth's and Heaven's bright and shining beauty?" Proserpina laughed mirthlessly, took the box, and turned away. I could not see what she put in.

"Thank you. Now I must go."

"Goodbye, then." She sighed deeply, as though she wished that autumn and winter were over and she were free to leave the Underworld with me.

XIV ⚭

Thanks to the sop, the coin, and forbearance, I made my way back safely.

Emerging from the crater, I saw myriad colors playing in the autumn light. I drew deep breaths of fragrant air, and looked and looked insatiably about—at rocks, each one inimitably shaped; at trees, their graceful branches, leafless now, reaching upward as though praising the sky with its incomparable blue and its ever-changing clouds.

I too reached upward, offering thanks to Jupiter and to all the gods who preserve and share this world with us mortals. I thanked Mercury especially.

Then I remembered my old nurse advising, "To speed your prayers to the gods' ears, close your eyes." But when I closed them, the grim specters that had reached out in vain to me below reappeared in my inner vision. Now I was free to let pity back into my heart, and I wept a flood of tears for all those wretched souls.

I stood at the edge of a small round pond. My tears fell in the pond and made ripples that spread out into wide and wider circles.

When my tears ceased and the pond grew still, I saw a tattered creature looking up at me, a dismal, bedraggled woman with bleary eyes, sunken cheeks, cracked, sore lips, hair hanging down in clumps.

She was myself: the Psyche who, when small, had splotched mud on her face and stuck burrs in her hair to make herself plain, the Psyche who, later, had won the love of Amor with her beauty.

"Oh, Amor!" I cried aloud, and threw myself on the ground. Pan's words in my ears, "Win him back," were a mockery to me now.

Even if I had all the lip balms, eye and cheek paints, creams and lotions known to womankind at my disposal, I could never, never hope to re-claim my beauty.

Oh, but . . . in my hand all this while was the ivory box containing Queen Proserpina's magic. . . .

The lid was tightly shut. I well remembered Mercury's warning. But what had I to lose? What greater misfortune could still come to me than the loss of Amor and his love for me?

I opened the box the tiniest bit. I meant to borrow just one grain or two of the magic. But before I could slip my finger in, out wafted a mist. It started as the slenderest wisp, and grew and grew. Soon it enfolded the rocks, the trees, the very sky above.

It wrapped me in its whiteness.

I could no longer move my limbs, or speak, or weep, even for the baby now never to be born.

My senses failed. The whiteness in whose thrall I lay hid everything from view—except for one small, curious creature on the ground beside me. I saw it creep forth from a shroudlike sheath. It opened golden wings and flew away. It was the butterfly who bears my name. I wished that it were I.

Then I consigned my soul to Mercury to guide to the realm of the dead.

A kiss returned my lips to life.

My senses reawakened.

"Stygian sleep, yield up your power!" I heard my splendid husband shout. I saw him leap, warriorlike, at the whiteness.

He struck it more hard blows, and faster, than a hailstorm pelts the ground with hail. He butted it, kicked holes in it, ripped and gashed it from all directions till it hung from the trees and over the crater and all around in giant, jagged shreds.

Quickly he gathered up the shreds, squeezed them together, made them dwindle into one slender wisp, which he forced back into the box, and clamped the lid down tight.

Then, oh, then, we embraced.

"Love, forgive me," I said, touching his shoulder where the oil had spilled.

"I have done so a thousand times over. The wound has healed. You have more than made amends, my Psyche. It's I who ask forgiveness."

"You? Whatever for?"

"All you endured for love of me while I lay weak and helpless on my mother's bed."

"Let it be forgotten. What restored your strength, my Amor?"

"You, Psyche. Your image in my dreams. The Psyche I first saw sitting on the stone bench in your father's garden. The Psyche of our magic nights in our magic dwelling—"

"The one who held the knife and shone the lamp on you?"

"Yes, that Psyche, too. Your face, your voice grew ever clearer, till I could no longer bear to be apart from you. Then I arose from my mother's bed and became my rightful self, your Amor." He gazed so intensely at my face, I grew ashamed and covered it with my hands.

"Psyche, do not hide from me." He moved my hands away. "How beautiful you are!"

"No, do not mock me. I know how I look. I saw my reflection in the pond."

"Mock you? Oh, my dearest, in all my searching, I saw no sight that can compare with you." He waved his hand over the pond, commanding the water to be still. "Look in the pond again."

I did. This time I saw my love for him, and his for me, shining from my eyes.

"Are you content?" he asked.

"Yes. Oh, yes!"

We lay down side by side. He touched the roundness of my belly. "I traveled far," he said. "Now let me rest where bliss is."

He placed his cheek there. Just then the child inside me stirred. "Oh, wonder!" Amor cried aloud. "Oh, joy I never knew!"

I asked, "Now can we be always together?"

"Not yet." He stood up, helped me up, too. "We must leave each other one more time. We both still have tasks before us. Yours is to bring this box back to Venus as she bid you." He placed it in my hands. "Let no more harm come from it."

"What must *you* do? Where will you go?"

"To Mount Olympus, where the gods hold council, to plead our cause, yours and mine." He kissed me once more on the lips. "Soon, my beloved," he whispered. Then he took wing and soared into the sky.

I returned to Venus.

"How well you look, considering where you have been," she said. "But you have kept me waiting much too long. I must hurry and repair my appearance. I am awaited on Olympus. Quick, give me the box."

She snatched it from me. Her fingers touched the lid.

"Beware!" I cried.

But what power had I to prevent her from opening it?

XV

High on Mount Olympus, seated on their gleaming thrones, Jupiter and Juno watched the deities arrive: Minerva, goddess of the arts and skills, an owl, her sacred bird, perched on her shoulder; proud Apollo, god of sunlight, music, and prophecy; his twin, bright-haired, lithe Diana, goddess of the hunt; Mercury, on winged sandals, holding his staff, the caduceus, to which two snakes, guardians of ancient secrets, clung; ivy-wreathed Bacchus, god of wine and revelry; Vesta, veiled and solemn goddess of the hearth and household piety; Ceres, dressed in mourning for her daughter, Proserpina, confined in Tartarus; lame, limping Vul-

can, god over fire and the forge; Mars, the strong, fierce war god, carrying his blood-bespattered spear.

Jupiter was disappointed. He flailed his thunderbolt about. "Where are Venus and Cupid?" he asked Mercury. "It is on their account this council meets. Why are they not here?"

Mercury made excuses for them. "Father, Venus wished to look her best for the occasion. She asks your patience awhile longer. Cupid also asks your patience—"

"I have been patient long enough," Jupiter complained. "I miss the grace, the elegance Venus brings to our gatherings—"

"You miss Cupid even more," Juno whispered in his ear. "You can't wait till he arouses some lewd, adulterous appetite in you."

"Not lewd, dear wife." But yes, Jupiter would gladly have felt the quickening of desire in his blood once more, and he thought longingly of his past conquests. . . .

Of the maiden Europa, playfully stroking the snow-white bull, trustingly climbing on his back, not suspecting it was he till he plunged into the waves and swam across the sea with her. . . . Of the titaness Latona, on whom he had fathered Apollo and Diana. . . . Of the naiad Maia in her cave in Arcadia, who bore him Mercury. . . . *Of queenly Alcmene, in whose womb he had engendered Hercules. . . . And of young Prince Ganymede, once an earthling, now his cupbearer. . . . Of Leda, who'd accepted him in swan shape. . . . Oh, and countless others, going far, far back, to long before he'd married his sister, Juno. . . .*

Whom he now reminded, "After each desire cooled, I faithfully returned to you."

"Faithfully?" *She raised an eyebrow. She pushed her throne closer to his, the better to rebuke him out of earshot.*

The others, too, muttered impatiently over the absent Cupid and Venus. With son and mother gone for such a time, life for many of them on Olympus had grown tedious. What, they wondered, was missing?

"Passion," *Apollo said.*

"The drunkenness that comes not from wine," *Bacchus said.*

"Hunger for conquest," *said Mars.*

"Lustful mischief," *said Vulcan, shaking a fist at Mars, for he was still angry that Venus, while Vulcan's wife, had made Mars her lover.*

Juno had overheard. She said to the assemblage, "I'll tell you what I miss: devotion of the sort that outlasts infatuation and unites two beings in a lasting bond."

Vesta said, "I miss it, too. I do not see much evidence of such devotion in these times."

"Nor I. But then devotion never was among the feelings that Venus or her son ignites," said silver-eyed Minerva.

"I for one don't miss them," said Diana, rising to her feet. "I have all I could wish for." And she spoke in praise of living singly, hunting with her companions through the woodlands she held dear, doing as she chose.

Apollo pulled at her tunic, suggesting she sit down, and said in a superior tone, "Sister, you know nothing of the feelings Venus and Cupid enkindle."

"Because I am a virgin? Respect me for that. It is a rare distinction, well worth preserving."

"Yes, and all the more reason why Venus and Cupid are needed to ignite new passions. Or else all young gods and humans would stay virgins. Then virginity would soon be commonplace and lose all its distinction."

Diana's pine green eyes flashed anger. "You argue cleverly, my brother. But this whole matter is your fault."

"My fault? Whatever can you mean?"

"Your Pythoness began it all, the one at Miletus, with her demented prattle."

" 'Demented prattle'? Mind how you speak of her!

Twin though you are to me, do not presume too much upon my patience. The Pythoness is sacred. Her prophecies, when understood, are deepest truth."

"Also the one about the 'dragon bridegroom,' whom even we gods fear?" Diana laughed. "Surely that was a smoke screen for the benefit of shameful little Cupid while he indulged his fancy for the human princess and had his little fling?"

" 'Shameful little Cupid'? He is mightier than you can know, and dragonlike indeed, inflicting pain without cause or warning. We do right to fear him. The arrow stings of love can wound as sharply as any dragon's teeth or claws—"

A rush of wings stopped Apollo in midspeech. Suddenly the son of Venus stood tall and strong before him, and his voice rang out, melodious, with new authority:

"Apollo, you spoke true. I was dragonlike when I was Cupid. I cared not what havoc my arrows inflicted. I ask your pardon, and all your pardons, gods and goddesses, for the pain that as Cupid I caused. Know that I am changed. I am Amor now. My bride, the princess Psyche, gave the name to me."

He turned to Jupiter and bowed. "Mighty ruler, you who guard the sacredness of oaths, I hereby swear before you, by my new name and all it signifies: may I forfeit immortality and join the lifeless throngs down

105

by the river Styx if ever in all eternity I break faith with loving Psyche."

Then not a sound was heard in the great council hall. For winds and storms were not allowed to blow around the palace, or rain or hail to pelt its roof. And all the gods and goddesses sat astonished, mute.

Juno broke the silence: "An ardent oath, and worthy of your new name, Amor. But answer me this: How can you, a god, speak of all eternity when proposing to love a human who eventually must die?"

"Goddess, hear me. Never did any human or immortal strive more nobly or bravely for love than did Psyche." He told of the enormous tasks she had accomplished, of her descent to the Underworld and of her return. "Great Juno, picture Psyche, justly famed for her great beauty, catching sight of her reflection, pale, begrimed, exhausted utterly. Imagine her, after heeding all the warnings, succumbing to despair, and against all better wisdom, opening the forbidden box—"

"A very human thing to do," Juno remarked.

"Yes, but don't you see? It is to her very humanity that I owe the godhood you now recognize. By her own example, Psyche has led me to my truest self. Boundless was her love for me, and boundless now is mine for her. I beseech you, grant us acknowledgment—and this one favor. . . ."

Juno, greatly moved, knew what Amor was asking. The whole assemblage knew.

"I alone have power to grant it," said Jupiter, rattling the thunderbolt.

"Then do. You granted it to Ganymede and to Hercules, both times against my will. This time I wish it," Juno urged.

Amor bowed to Jupiter and pleaded, "I ask this boon for Psyche's sake and mine, and for all true lovers' sakes for all of time to come: let Psyche be immortal."

Jupiter furrowed his brow. He thought hard and long, then called Minerva to his side. "Daughter, wise one, sprung from my own head, advise me. Shall I, by commingling human with divine, diminish all our godhood?"

"Or, rather, exalt what is valiant and good in humans?" asked Minerva in reply. She smoothed away the wrinkles from his forehead and gave her advice by taking his hand and placing it over his heart.

Then all the gods and goddesses awaited Jupiter's decision.

XVI ⚜

When I returned once more to Venus's domain,
I implored her, "Beware, immortal goddess, do
not open the box!"

"You tell me to beware? And what I should
not do?" She broke into chilling laughter. "Beware of finding the box empty? Because you stole
the beauty it contained?"

She moved to open it.

"No, please!" I placed my hands on her wrists.

"How dare you touch me?"

"To keep you from harm." I knelt down before her. "I beg you to believe me: the box con-

tains a deathlike Stygian sleep. If you release it, it will overcome you and wrap you in its endlessness—"

"Why do you warn me, then? If that happened, you would be avenged for my cruelty to you. Tell me the truth: would you not find that sweet?"

I felt no throbbing in the hollow place behind my ear. I answered, "No. I would not find it sweet if, engulfed in an eternal sleep, you could never again see your son, whom you and I both love." I stood up then, my belly protruding. "And if you never saw the child I soon will bear, who will resemble you, and its father, Amor—"

" 'Amor'? Presumptuous mortal, did you give a new name to the son I bore?"

She stepped close. She raised her arm and would have struck me down—but for a blaze of light in which a god appeared between us. I knew him by his winged sandals, by the *caduceus*, and by his likeness to the face on the signpost at the crossroads. It was Mercury.

He caressed her cheek. "Venus, always dear to me," he said, "you have tarried too long on earth. Jupiter commands your presence in the council hall. He has things to tell you that will make you glad—I promise."

He waved his staff, and the doors of the coach house opened. A chariot of burnished gold rolled out.

He made a summoning motion with his hand and a cooing sound with his lips. At once four snow-white doves came flying and harnessed themselves to the chariot.

"Go now, Sister. Jupiter grows impatient."

Venus climbed in. The doves winged away.

"Have no fear," said Mercury. He flung one arm around me, swung me up as easily as if I, with my burden, were feather-light, and carried me through immeasurable heights of blueness to a tall gate of billowing clouds.

He touched the gate with his staff. It opened.

He covered my eyes with his arm lest my human vision shatter at the wonders in the place we entered.

I heard music pouring forth a wealth of tones and harmonies.

Mercury said, "That is my brother Apollo playing the *cithara*."

110

I heard flute sounds and the voices of goddesses singing. Mercury said, "Those are my sisters, the Muses."

Behind and amidst the music, I heard the almost silent sounds of airy fabric rustling, of feet barely touching the floor.

Mercury said, "Those are the Graces dancing."

Then, close by, I heard the velvet-smooth gliding of liquid into a vessel.

"That is Jupiter's cupbearer, Ganymede, filling your cup," said Mercury.

I felt a cup held to my lips.

I drank. I drained the cup. I stayed as I had always been, yet was transformed. The liquid, the music, the dancing all became a part of me as I became my truest self, made jubilant and new.

"That was nectar you drank, our godly sustenance here on Olympus. Now you are one of us," said Mercury, and lifted his arm from my eyes.

With a clarity of vision greater than exists on earth, I saw Amor, exultant, coming toward me.

"Always, always," sang the moment, sang our eyes and hearts.

All the gods and goddesses—save Venus—

welcomed me in their midst. Venus stood alone, saying not a word.

Jupiter motioned her to him and assured her, "All is well. You are the fairest goddess. You were from the day you arose from the sea, and you always will be. Your worshipers flock to your temples in great numbers once again. Psyche, immortal, will take not a whit away from the honors that are due you. Be comforted, my dear." He kissed her full on the lips and made her smile.

Then Venus came to us.

"Amor, my son . . ." She touched him on the forehead. "Can we be reconciled?"

For answer, Amor took her hand and placed it in mine. She kept it there and called me "Daughter."

Then she joined the Graces and, to everyone's delight, led them in a new dance.

Amor and I stood entwined. Our wedding feast began.

XVII ⚭

Psyche's father seldom went out among his people anymore. His sole companions were his books. Sometimes
they comforted him in his loneliness. But they had no
answers to the questions that troubled him: was he not
a good man, and a wise king? Then why had the gods
deprived him of what he treasured most?

One starry night, fragrant with the scent of almond
blossoms, for it was spring now, the old king had a
dream:

His youngest daughter floated in through the window.

"Dearest Father, see what I have brought you."

She put a bundle in his lap, wrapped in cloud-soft linen.

Two shining eyes in a small face looked seriously up at him, as though to memorize his features, then smiled so radiant a smile, it turned the whole bedchamber bright as noon.

"This is your granddaughter," Psyche said.

A warmth spread through the old king such as he had not felt since he had held the newly born Psyche in his arms. He said, "This child will live forever."

Then Psyche told him all that had happened since their parting on the mountaintop.

He listened while rocking the child. And he asked, "What is her name?"

"Hedonia. It comes from an ancient language known to all in Heaven."

"I also know it. My old teacher taught it to me when I was a boy," said the grandfather-king, smiling at the baby. "Hedonia, my darling, newest goddess, your name means pleasure, joy, and bliss—all of which are mine, now that you have come." And he kissed her lily-petal cheeks.

* * *

Next morning, the king asked that Psyche's old nurse be brought to him.

She came hobbling along on her cane.

He told her the dream.

She listened with her eyes closed. His dream appeared on the insides of her eyelids exactly as the king described it, and she said, "Yes, that's how it had to be."

She started humming a tune that she'd sung to Psyche years ago. It had a lively beat. She let her cane drop to the floor, took the king by the hands, and they danced around the room together—hopping, skipping as though they'd both grown young again.

Later that morning, the king went to visit the temple of Venus. He placed a large bouquet on the altar. But one flower, blue as the sky, and with a radiant center, he put into the goddess-statue's hand. Then he wondered, Am I back in the dream? He could have sworn the statue smiled at him.

"Well, of course she did. I hope you smiled back," the nurse said, rocking her arms as if they were a cradle. "You have a lot to smile about, you two."

*   *   *

That same day, the king sent for the best architects and builders in the land. And soon a glorious new temple, the temple of Psyche, Amor, and Hedonia, stood atop the mountain where this story began.

Doris Orgel
has written forty-nine books for young people,
among them her well-known *The Devil in Vienna*,
Nobodies and Somebodies, and *Risking Love*. The most
recently published, also inspired by her love of
mythology, is *Ariadne, Awake!* illustrated by
Barry Moser. She lives in New York City.